WITHDRAWN

A Very Sticky Situation

by Noel Gyro Potter
illustrated by Joseph Cannon

HUNTINGTON CITY TOWNSHIP
PUBLIC LIBRARY
255 WEST PARK DRIVE
HUNTINGTON, IN 46750

visit us at www.abdopublishing.com

To JG, my BFF, the husband and father I only dreamt existed,
and to the other three loves in my life. . .
having you to love is all that matters to me. — NGP

Published by Magic Wagon, a division of the ABDO Publishing Group, 8000 West 78th Street, Edina, Minnesota 55439. Copyright © 2009 by Abdo Consulting Group, Inc. International copyrights reserved in all countries. All rights reserved. No part of this book may be reproduced in any form without written permission from the publisher.
Looking Glass Library™ is a trademark and logo of Magic Wagon.

Printed in the United States.

Written by Noel Gyro Potter
Illustrations by Joseph Cannon
Edited by Stephanie Hedlund and Rochelle Baltzer
Interior layout and design by Neil Klinepier
Cover design by Neil Klinepier

Library of Congress Cataloging-in-Publication Data
Potter, Noel Gyro.
 A very sticky situation / written by Noel Gyro Potter ; illustrated by Joseph Cannon.
   p. cm. -- (The adventures of Marshall & Art)
 ISBN 978-1-60270-201-1
 [1. Karate--Fiction. 2. Bullies--Fiction. 3. Friendship--Fiction.] I. Cannon, Joseph, 1958- ill. II. Title.
 PZ7.P8553Ve 2008
 [E]--dc22
                                                                  2008003624

"Boys, time for breakfast!" Marshall's mom, Marti, yelled.

"Be right there, Mom!" shouted Marshall.

"I'm starving! What's for breakfast?" asked Marshall's younger brother Art as he flew down the stairs.

Marshall and Art's family was already in the kitchen. Their youngest brother, Harley, was playing with the family cats, Kata and Kumite. Their dad, karate champion Johnny James, sat quietly reading the paper.

Johnny and Marti taught classes at their karate studio, where Marshall and Art had earned their black belts. Johnny and Marti were very proud of their sons. The black belt brothers felt pretty proud of themselves, too.

Once Marshall, Art, and Harley were seated, Marti said, "Boys, your father and I need a favor from you. Our new neighbor, Mrs. Gates, would like you two to walk home with her son, Brian."

"Mom, do you mean Brian 'Bubble Gum' Gates?" asked Art.

"'Bubble Gum'? Why 'Bubble Gum'?" asked Marti.

"Because he's always chewing a gigantic mouthful of gum," said Art. "Some kids at recess were calling him 'Bubble Gum' and he didn't seem to mind."

"Are you sure about that?" Johnny asked. "I remember Marshall telling us that Billy Bailey called him names that he didn't like."

"Billy used to call me 'Marshmallow Marshall'," Marshall said. He quietly thought about how Billy and his boys laughed as they yelled it. What made Marshall even more frustrated was whenever he would ask Billy to stop, Billy would just do it more.

"And how did it make you feel?" asked Johnny.

"I felt embarrassed and kind of mad," said Marshall.

"Billy always calls me 'Smarty Arty'," Art declared. "It made me want to teach that kid a thing or two! I still could, you know!"

"Boys, just because someone calls us names, doesn't mean it's true. But it always makes us feel bad, doesn't it? It's definitely not a cool thing to do and even worse, it's bullying," explained Johnny.

"I bet no one has ever bullied you," Marshall said proudly.

"That's not true, Marshall. I was picked on all the time when I was your age," said Johnny.

"What did you do about it, Dad? Did you pound the kids that made fun of you?" Art asked eagerly. He couldn't believe his karate-champion dad had been picked on.

"Boys, you've learned that fighting doesn't solve anything. Besides, bullies usually pick on the kids who are easy to bully. In order for bullies to feel strong or important, they want the other kids to be afraid of them," explained their dad.

HUNTINGTON CITY TOWNSHIP
PUBLIC LIBRARY
255 WEST PARK DRIVE
HUNTINGTON, IN 46750

"All right, we'll walk Brian home. Can we stop by the karate studio and show him around?" Art asked.

"That's a great idea! Now go, before you're both late for school!" Marti said. The boys hurried out the door.

During the walk to school, Art said, "I wish you could just fight that Billy and really teach him a lesson!"

"Using our karate to show off or to hurt others wouldn't be right. That's not why we got our black belts. I'll meet you and Brian after school," Marshall said as the bell rang.

When school let out, Marshall was nervous. He could see Art and Brian waiting for him.

"Hey, Brian, I'm Marshall! Are you guys ready to go?" he asked.

"I guess so. But are you sure it's okay for me to go to your parents' karate studio?" Brain asked. Then he began blowing a giant bubble.

The brothers were mesmerized by the size of it!

The boys had barely made it past the school when they saw Billy and his band of bullies.

"Uh-oh! I don't like this!" said Brian. "I think we should run."

"Trust us," said Marshall. "We know what we're doing."

19

As Billy got closer, he shouted, "Well, if it isn't Big Bubble Gum Belly Brian! Where's the bubble gum I told you to get me, Bubble Gum Face?"

"I-I-I didn't see you at school, but I-I-I can give you a piece now," stammered Brian. He was so scared he had stopped chewing his wad of gum and just stared at Billy.

"Brian doesn't have to give you any of his bubble gum, Billy. I guess you'll just have to buy your own," Marshall said.

"Yeah!" added Art. "Get your own bubble gum, Billy! Now, step out of our way. Our dad is waiting for us at our karate studio."

At that moment, Billy's friends realized that Marshall and Art were Johnny James's sons and black belts!

"Hey, Billy, I just remembered that I, um, have to watch my baby sister this afternoon," said one of Billy's buddies.

"Yeah, I gotta go, too! My mom really doesn't like it when I'm late!" said another.

"Go on, leave, you chickens! I don't need you. I never did!" Billy yelled at his friends.

Suddenly, Billy found himself outnumbered. He said to Brian, "For the last time, are you going to give me my gum, or do I have to beat it out of you?"

Marshall stepped in and snapped back, "The answer is still NO, Billy. And you're not going to beat it out of anyone."

"And who's going to stop me . . . you, Marshmallow?" Billy said.

"That's up to you, Billy," answered Marshall.

Not feeling brave with his friends gone, Billy thought if he pushed Brian down, he could run away. He stepped toward Brian.

Brian was so scared he just stood there with his mouth wide open! A big glob of bubble gum fell from his mouth. It landed on the sidewalk with a loud, soggy splat!

Billy stepped right on the gooey bubble gum. "Whoa! Look out!" hollered Billy, his arms waving wildly in the air.

Marshall and Art quickly took action! Marshall stepped left and Art stepped right. They each grabbed one of Billy's arms, saving him just as he was about to fall crashing to the ground!

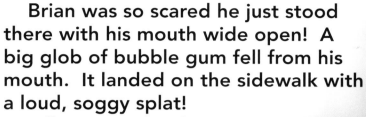

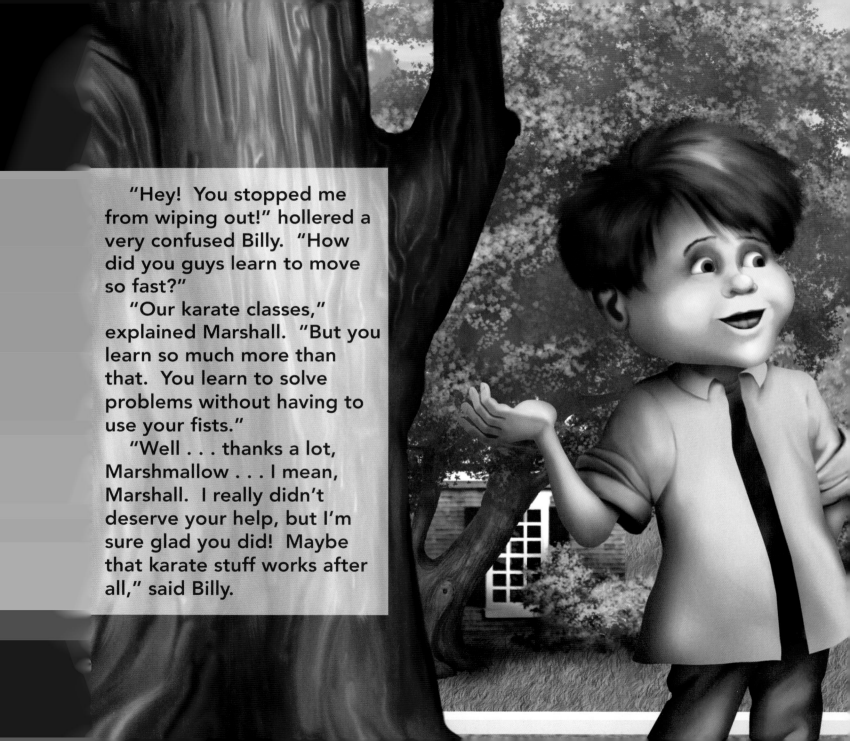

"Hey! You stopped me from wiping out!" hollered a very confused Billy. "How did you guys learn to move so fast?"

"Our karate classes," explained Marshall. "But you learn so much more than that. You learn to solve problems without having to use your fists."

"Well . . . thanks a lot, Marshmallow . . . I mean, Marshall. I really didn't deserve your help, but I'm sure glad you did! Maybe that karate stuff works after all," said Billy.

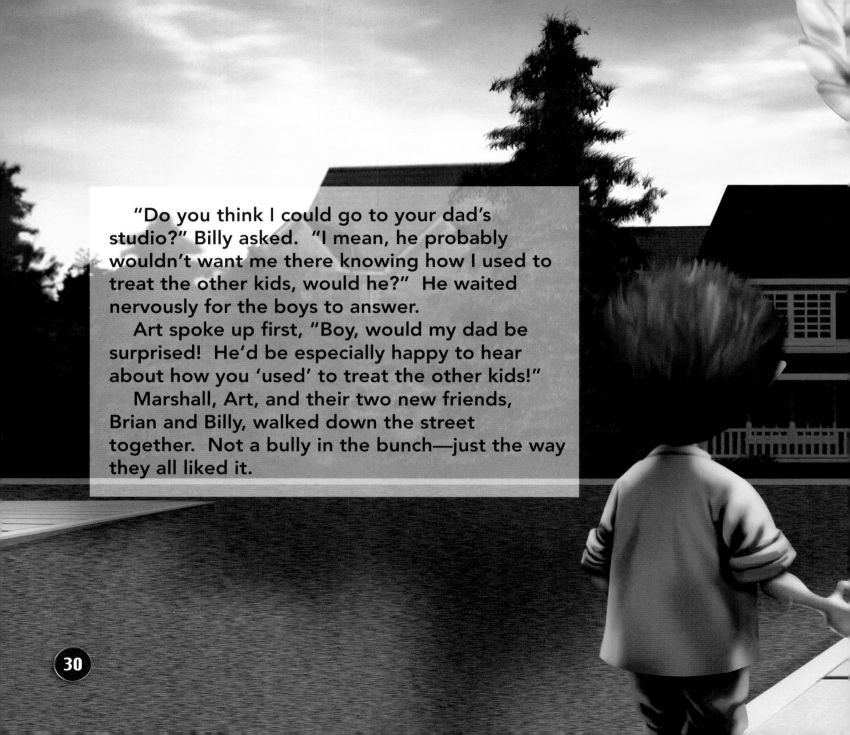

"Do you think I could go to your dad's studio?" Billy asked. "I mean, he probably wouldn't want me there knowing how I used to treat the other kids, would he?" He waited nervously for the boys to answer.

Art spoke up first, "Boy, would my dad be surprised! He'd be especially happy to hear about how you 'used' to treat the other kids!"

Marshall, Art, and their two new friends, Brian and Billy, walked down the street together. Not a bully in the bunch—just the way they all liked it.

Tips for Dealing with Bullies

Bullies have been around since the beginning of time. A common bully tactic is to threaten, hurt, or insult others while going unnoticed and undetected. Learning how to handle bullying is key to stopping it.

Children:
- Tell an adult when you are threatened or hurt by another person. Do not let a bully frighten you into not telling.
- Even though you may be afraid, show you are strong and brave. Stand up to a bully like Marshall did in this story and say, "I won't let you treat me this way."
- Bullies usually pick on individuals, not groups. If you are being bullied, stay close to your friends.
- Find an adult you trust, such as a parent, guardian, teacher, or coach, that you can talk to about everything. Tell them about the good and bad things in your day.

Adults:
- Instill self-esteem and confidence in children by listening to them and encouraging them to trust and confide in you.
- Regularly remind children to report their encounters with a bully to an adult.
- Communicate with other parents, teachers, and administrators.
- Above all else, be informed. Volunteer in your child's classroom and on the playground to see what is happening there, and take time to ask about your child's day and listen to the answer.